This book belongs to

. . . .

LADYBIRD BOOKS

UK | USA | Canada | Ireland | Australia | India | New Zealand | South Africa

Ladybird Books is part of the Penguin Random House group of companies
whose addresses can be found at global.penguinrandomhouse.com.

www.penguin.co.uk   www.puffin.co.uk   www.ladybird.co.uk

Penguin
Random House
UK

First published 2017
008

Printed in China

A CIP catalogue record for this book is available from the British Library

ISBN: 978-0-241-29456-7

All correspondence to:
Ladybird Books
Penguin Random House Children's
80 Strand, London WC2R 0RL

Peppa Goes to London

Once upon a time, Peppa and her playgroup went on a day trip to London. When they arrived, Madame Gazelle told everyone to gather round.
"Children," she said, "this is London!"

"Wow!" gasped Peppa. "It's so busy."
London was a **very** big and **very** busy city.
There was so much to see that Madame Gazelle
couldn't decide where to go first.

Miss Rabbit had an idea.

"My friend the Queen lives in London," she said. "Maybe she can help . . ."

The Queen's house is called
Buckingham Palace.
Miss Rabbit went up to the
front gate and rang the bell.

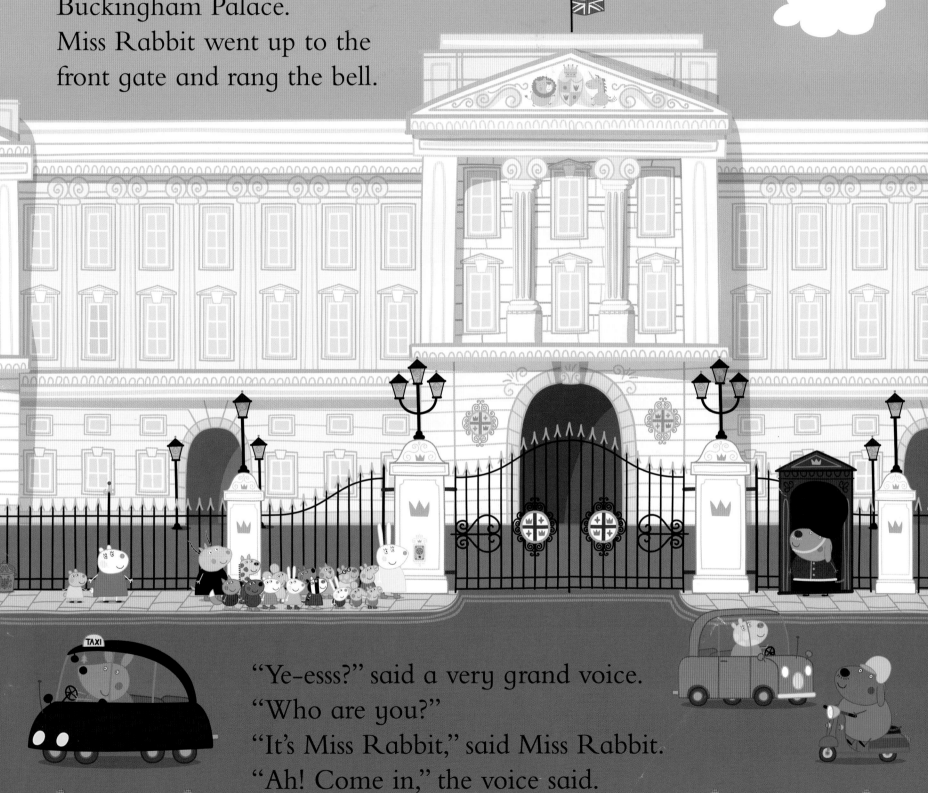

"Ye-esss?" said a very grand voice.
"Who are you?"
"It's Miss Rabbit," said Miss Rabbit.
"Ah! Come in," the voice said.

The voice belonged to the Queen.
"Hello, everyone," she said.
"Hello, Queen!" shouted the children.
"We're visiting London for the day,"
said Peppa, "but we don't know where to go."

"London is my city," said the Queen.
"I shall give you a guided tour!"

Hooray!

Hee!
Hee!

Hee!
Hee!

The Queen led Peppa and her friends out on to the street.
She flagged down a bright red bus.

"Mr Driver," she said, "please may we borrow your bus?"
"You must be joking!" sniffed the driver.
"No," replied the Queen. "I am your queen."

The driver helped everyone
on to the bus. If the Queen
asks you to do something,
you must do it!

Peppa had never been on a bus
like this before.
"It has stairs in it!" she gasped.
The Queen showed the children
up to the top deck. From up
there, they could see everything.

Ting! Ting!
The bus set off.
"First stop, Big Ben!"
said the Queen.

The bus stopped in front of Big Ben.

"Big Ben is a clock tower," said the Queen.
"It helps us tell the time."
Edmond Elephant shook his head.
"Actually Big Ben is the bell *inside*,
not the tower itself."

Dong! Dong! Dong!

Edmond knew a lot
for a little elephant.
Edmond was a clever clogs.

"That was loud," exclaimed Danny Dog. "That is the sound of Big Ben telling us the time," said the Queen. "It rang three times, so it is three o'clock."

Dong!
Dong!
Dong!

Dong!
Dong!
Dong!

Dong!
Dong!
Dong!

Pedro Pony had a question.
"If the clock rang six times,
would that make it six o'clock?"
"Yes, it would," said the Queen.

Dong! Dong! Dong! Dong! Dong! Dong! Dong! Dong! Dong!

Dong! Dong! Dong! Dong! Dong! Dong! Dong!

"And if it rang a hundred
times?" he wondered.
"Then it would be
broken," said the Queen.
"Oh," said Pedro.

The Queen drove the bus to Tower Bridge.

"Stop!" shouted the bridge keeper. "You can't cross here."
The Queen was not amused. "Why not?" she asked.

"I'm sorry, Your Majesty," said the bridge keeper, "but a ship needs to pass under the bridge."

The bridge lifted up just in time.
The ship sailed through.

"Good," said the Queen. "Now we can be on our way. Please lower the bridge."
The bridge keeper shook her head.
Another ship was coming!

The Queen wanted to get going – Peppa and her friends couldn't wait around all day! **"Hold tight, everyone!"** she cried.

Wheeeee

eeeeeeee!

The bus zoomed on to the
bridge and then – crunk!
– it got stuck in the middle.
"Now what do we do?"
asked Miss Rabbit.

"Everybody move to the front of the bus," ordered the Queen.
"One . . .
two . . .
three . . ."

"Go!" shouted Peppa.

The bus started to tip and wobble . . .

Cr-eeeak!

. . . then **vroomed** down the other side of the bridge!

Hooray! The Queen was *very* good at driving buses.

"Are you enjoying the tour?" asked the Queen.
"YES, YOUR MAJESTY!" bellowed the children.

"Open-top buses are the best," said Peppa.
"Why aren't all buses like this?"

A raindrop fell on her head. Drip! Drop! Plop!
That was why.
"Children!" said Madame Gazelle. "Open your umbrellas."

The bus chugged through the rain to Trafalgar Square.
"Oh dear," sighed the Queen.
"What a shame! It's full of puddles."

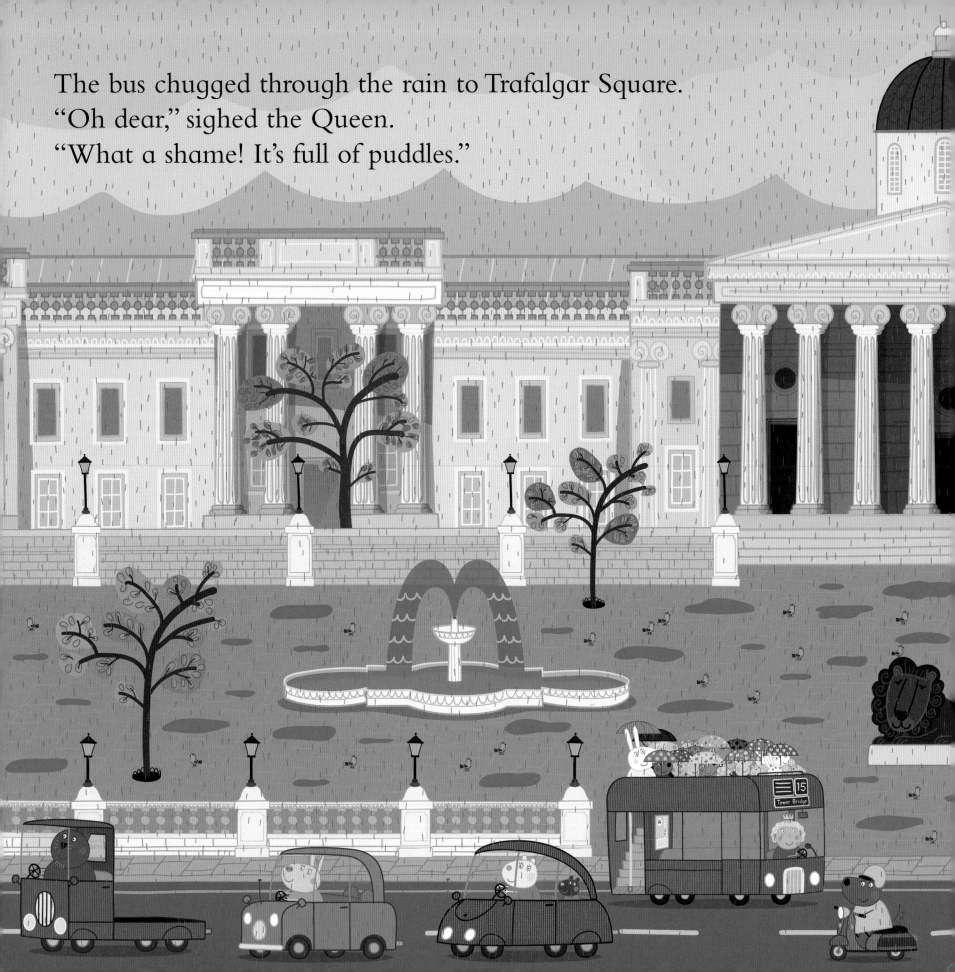

The Queen was right. There were puddles everywhere!
She frowned. "I think our tour is over."
"Awwwww!" groaned the children as they climbed off the bus.

Hee!

Splosh!

Peppa jumped in a puddle.
George jumped in a puddle.
Then everyone jumped in a puddle!

Splash!

Hee!

"We love puddles!" shouted the children. "Come and splash, Your Majesty," called Peppa. "It's fun!"

Splish!

"Why not!" said the Queen.
"One is wearing one's boots."

The Queen loves jumping in London puddles.
Everyone loves jumping in London puddles!